Roshni
Children's Books

UNESCO WORLD HERITAGE SITES OF INDIA SERIES

United Nations
Educational, Scientific and
Cultural Organization

Chhatrapati Shivaji Terminus
Travelling through Time

Author **Subuhi Jiwani**
Artist **Kishan Dev**

MAPIN PUBLISHING

"The clocks are my babies," Bandu often says.

He has cared for time machines at the Chhatrapati Shivaji Maharaj Terminus for almost 40 years. Every morning, he begins his rounds on the ground floor of the grand station building. He moves in a clockwise direction, from one pendulum clock to another, until he reaches the granddaddy of them all. It's ten feet wide, in a large attic above the second floor.

Today is a muggy summer's day, and Bandu is exhausted from the winding and the climbing. He sets out for the sugarcane juice stall a few yards from the station. Once there, he asks for a large glass. As soon as the juice touches his lips, he only hears one sound: gulp, gulp, g u l p... Relief at last.

Before he has finished, he sees Laali and Mithu standing in a corner, staring at his glass of juice with desiring eyes. They are too shy to ask for some. Bandu gestures with his hands: *do you want some*?

They give him wide smiles, and soon, he's ordering two more glasses.

As Laali, the older of the two, and Mithu are slurping their juice, Bandu asks them, "What are you doing here? And where are your parents?"

"They work over there," Laali speaks up, pointing to a construction site nearby. "There's no one to take care of us at home so we come with them."

"But we get bored!" Mithu complains. "So we roam, roam, roam but get tired and thirsty."

Wiping her lips, Laali says, "We saw this beautiful palace from far away and wondered whose it was..."

Bandu's eyes almost pop out of their sockets. "Palace? Oh no! This is no palace. It is one of the grandest train stations in India and the world! The Chhatrapati Shivaji Maharaj Terminus!"

KISHAN DEV.

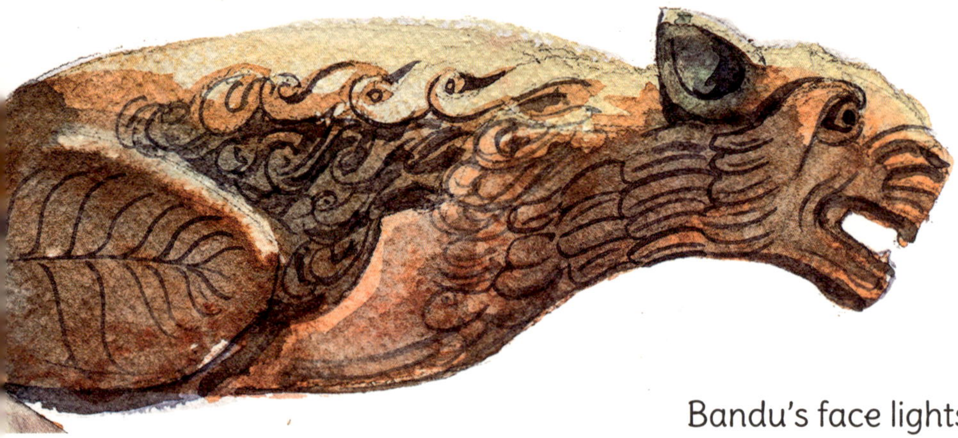

Bandu's face lights up when he talks about the station. His first job was as CST's clock keeper, and it will be his last. He treasures the building like a second home.

"Can we go inside?" Mithu wants to know.

"Umm..." Bandu wavers. Only people who work with the railways or tourists who pay an entry fee are allowed inside this fancy building. Bandu would like to show Laali and Mithu its many arches and animals. But would he get caught?

Lost in thought, Bandu feels someone tugging at his shirt. It's Mithu, looking up at him. "Please, please, please!" Mithu begs.

"All right." Bandu has thought of a way. "There's a secret passage that no one takes. Come, but you must be quiet."

They walk towards the bus depot on the south side of the building. Between two bus stops is a small, unlocked gate. Before opening it, Bandu glances at Laali and Mithu, his finger on his lips. Quietly, they step inside.

They walk through a maze of arches, past circular staircases, around pillars with creatures looking down at them.

"Who are they?" Laali asks loudly, pointing to a string of birds.

"Sssshhh!" Bandu whispers.

On hearing footsteps behind them, Bandu sneaks Laali and Mithu into the railway museum on the ground floor. Far from being afraid, the children feel they've entered a playground.

On the wall is a photograph of a man with a moustache that covers his upper lip. "How does he eat?" Mithu chuckles.

Bandu frowns. "He's the man because of whom you're standing in this building. He designed it! He was the chief architect—Mr Stevens."

"Archi... who?" Laali looks puzzled.

Mithu, by now, has jumped across to the models of the first steam trains that pulled out of the station. Laali is quick to follow. They're both dazzled by the blinking lights inside a passenger coach.

"Never mind," Bandu says. He'd like to tell them about the history of the building. But how can he get them to pay attention and to listen?

He has an idea. "If you think the blinking lights are magical, wait till you see what I'm going to show you!" He pops his head out of the museum door and then back in. "All clear! Let's go!"

They run up two floors, a narrow spiral staircase and a wooden ladder. To the place he knows best—the clock room!

The gigantic clock makes their jaws drop. Bandu is reminded of the first time he saw it. He couldn't believe it was taller than him and that he had to climb a ladder to look at its insides.

Laali and Mithu run up this ladder and wait outside a door, behind which is the clock's motor. They can now hear the clock go *tick, tock, tick, tock...*

Bandu follows them up the ladder. Once on the landing, he opens a window. Now anyone can look out of the face of the clock! And Bandu invites Laali and Mithu to do just that.

They crawl up next to him and peer out the window. Outside, the city zooms past. "So, ready for some magic?" Bandu asks. They nod excitedly. With his entire strength, he pushes the clock's minute hand in the anti-clockwise direction.

A sudden whirring sound. The already bright sunlight becomes brighter. Cars moving on the main road become gray lines. People disappear. Everything speeds up.

In a fraction of a second, it's now a cloudy day. Horse-drawn carriages move on the cobbled street. Ladies in gowns walk along the pavements. And men in hats bow to each other.

They have travelled back in time!

It's 1880. The British rule India. Dadabhai Naoroji Road, which passes in front of CST, was then called Hornby Road. The 330-foot station building is under construction, and its dome is still being built.

From the window, Mithu spots a craftsman chiselling away at a big stone in the building's front yard. "Look!" he says with excitement, pointing to the man dressed in a turban and *dhoti*. "Can we go look at what he's doing?"

Bandu clutches Mithu's and Laali's hands, and they jump. They land close to the craftsman and watch him sculpt a funny-looking animal. "What's that, uncle?" Laali asks.

"It's a griffin," Bandu says. "A creature from myths, with the head and wings of an eagle and the body of a lion. It stands for strength and vigilance. Once the building is complete, it will be put above the second floor too!"

As they observe the craftsman, they realise that he's muttering under his breath. "Today, I long to see my children. I had to leave them behind in my village in Telengana and come to the city to work. Ah, life! Why must it be so difficult?"

The griffin, who is looking away from him, suddenly begins to speak!

"Life is difficult because that's just how it is! Imagine my plight! I'll be perched atop the building all my life, with no companions at all! But wise women and men have said we must be thankful for what we have and accept what comes our way. So I'm trying to make peace with things—as they are."

"What a beautiful thought, my friend!" the craftsman replies. "I hope the memory of our friendship takes you through your lonely hours."

The griffin closes its eyes.

"This is sad!" Mithu protests.

"Sad?" Bandu asks, confused. "Okay, let me show you another side of the building."

They fly back up towards the clock. This time, after turning the minute hand, they land in the 1930s.

They crash-land in the middle of noise, crowds and commotion! From the window in the face of the clock, they see men and women marching from the north towards CST. And they can hear songs of protest against the British Raj.

The protesters gather in front of CST. Just then, the clock strikes six and hordes of factory workers arrive at the station. The *satyagrahi*s hold up placards, distribute leaflets and talk to the workers about Mahatma Gandhi's message of non-violent resistance to British rule.

The minute hand has barely moved to the 15-minute mark when the police show up and start beating the protesters with sticks. "But they're not doing anything bad!" Laali cries.

"Yes, that's true," says Bandu, "except that the British rule India right now. And the people of our country don't want to be under them anymore."

"Won't they get hurt if the police hit them?" Mithu asks.

"Of course they will," Bandu says. "But they are willing to suffer pain for their cause. Gandhiji has told them to say 'No' to the British without raising so much as a finger."

Bandu is eager to tell Laali and Mithu as much about CST as he can. "In fact, when Gandhiji was arrested by the police in 1942 he was brought here, to this station. From here, he was made to take a train to Pune, where he was put under house arrest."

"You see," he continues with conviction, "much that is important took place in and around CST."

Bandu is about to begin another story when Mithu interrupts him. “Can we also go to tomorrow time?”

“Do you mean travel to the future?” Bandu asks. Mithu gives him three quick nods. “Well, yes! We sure can! Would you like to lean out of the window and push the minute hand with all your strength?”

Mithu looks scared but Laali says, “Don’t worry. I will hold you tight and not let you fall.”

So Mithu leans out, Laali grabs him at the waist and Bandu holds on to Laali. With all his strength and little hands, Mithu gives the minute hand a big push and it flies beyond his reach, rotating many, many times.

This time, it takes them to the year 2500.

What they see outside the clock window stuns them. Cars fly through the air, trains travel at the speed of sound, and people walk so fast their legs look like wheels. There are no trees and not a soul on the street; everyone is in cars or on skywalks. But CST is exactly the same—almost.

Bandu, Laali and Mithu are just about catching their breath, when a dog howls loudly. They scan the street but don't see any strays.

"Look above, towards the dome!" says a voice from somewhere. They turn 90 degrees and they're amazed by what they see. The gargoyles, or water-spouts carved from stone, just below the dome have sprung to life!

Bandu rubs his eyes to make sure he's really seeing this. "For what are they sending out this call?" he wonders aloud.

"A party, what else?" the voice from nowhere continues.

"But who are you?" Bandu asks, with a tinge of fear.

"I'm Gryphonita, whom you saw over 500 years ago talking to a craftsman," says the griffin as she leaves her position above the second floor and floats to where they are. In a few hundred years, the building's sculptures are flying! Bandu begins to look worried.

"We can now freely move around in the Virtual Zone. Meaning, our virtual selves can," she says. "And we can talk to each other over wireless networks."

"Woohoo!" Gryphonita hoots so loudly they have to plug their ears with their fingers. "Oh, sorry," she says. "I'm still learning to control my voice. I haven't spoken in several centuries..."

"Wait, if you're flying," Bandu asks Gryphonita, "does that mean the walls will fly off too? If they do, how will the building stand?" He is visibly disturbed.

"Oh come on!" she says, "Don't be so scared! Only our spirits are flying, not our actual bodies."

"Okay, okay... I don't completely understand how that is possible but I'm relieved," he says. "I was afraid the building would collapse!"

In the meantime, Laali's and Mithu's eyes have been flitting from him to Gryphonita and back.

Mithu, curious as he is, butts in. "Okay, so who all can fly?"

"Everyone, kid! Depends on who wants to," Gryphonita says. "Come, let's go meet everyone at the party! It's going to start anytime now. Use the red backlit bands on your wrists to access the Virtual Zone!"

They follow her directions and soon enough, they've left their physical bodies. They follow Gryphonita, who flies away from the clock room, through the second floor verandahs, down the central staircase into the central hall. The party is on!

All of the building's big and small sculptures are here — Progress, who stands above the dome; Jeejeebhoy and Shankerseth who built Asia's first passenger railway line that started from here; and all the gargoyles, griffins, monkeys, foxes, rams, owls, parrots and sparrows.

Not to be forgotten are the hundreds of species of vines that crawl over the walls and sprout leaves in niches. And Frederick William Stevens's photo from the museum joins them. Everyone is grooving to the beat, and Bandu, Laali and Mithu join in too!

Soon, Mithu begins to feel pangs of hunger and thirst. "What time is it?" he screams to Bandu over the din.

Bandu takes them to one side, near a standing pendulum clock. They huddle together so they can hear each other. "In which time?" he asks loudly, over the music. "This one or the one we left behind?"

"Our home time!" Mithu says impatiently. "It feels like dinner time because I'm starving," he complains. "Also, today is our *paani-puri* day and if we don't go back, we'll have to wait for one whole week before we can have it again!"

"Okay, okay..." Bandu reassures him. "Don't worry, you won't have to miss your *paani-puri*."

"We just don't want to be late!" says Laali. "I hope the *bhelpuriwallah* doesn't go away..."

"Relax. He won't, trust me," Bandu says. "Let's go home!"

Bandu reaches for Laali's and Mithu's hands and soon, they're circling up towards the dome and flying to the clock room. They find their bodies, merge with them, and Bandu gets ready to push the minute hand in the reverse direction.

"Ready?" he asks, as sister and brother shut their eyes tight. "Here we go!"

Before they can open them, the time has changed. They're back in 2018, in the clock room. The clock says 6 p.m., and they're supposed to meet their parents right now at the *bhelpuriwallah* opposite CST.

“Oh, we must rush,” Laali says, looking at the time. “Thanks for everything, uncle! We’ll keep coming to meet you.”

Mithu jumps in. “This was so much fun! We’ll always remember this day!”

They give Bandu a tight hug and then run out of the clock room, down the stairs, through the front yard and out the main gate. Their parents are waiting for them and smile as they see them coming. The *bhelpuriwallah* has two *puri*s full of tangy *paani* ready. Laali and Mithu open their mouths, and their mummy pops in these *puri*s.

They soak in the *paani-puri* yumminess and smile with their eyes. Behind them, at Chhatrapati Shivaji Maharaj Terminus, their inanimate friends, the gargoyles and griffins, are smiling with them.

Now it is *Your* Turn!

All Aboard the Heritage Express!

Plan a secret passage from your classroom to the playground that only you know about.

If you and your friends wanted to play some cricket without the teacher finding out, you could quickly go through the passage. Or if you were really hungry, you could quietly slip out to the canteen for a quick bite! What secret password would you and your friends use to guard the passage?

If there were a train from the Earth to Saturn, what celestial bodies would you see out the window during your journey?

There will be breakfast on the moon, lunch on Mars and some turbulence near the asteroid belt. Instead of railway crossings, the train will wait for comets to pass! What kind of food would you like to eat on this train journey?

If you could travel to the past, to which age would you go?

Would you go to the Jurassic age, with its large, roaring dinosaurs? Then you could find out how they died and come back to the present and win a Nobel Prize for your discovery! If you are a cricket fan, you could go to 1983 when India won the World Cup and watch the match live. Or you could go back a hundred years and say hello to your own great-grandmother when she was a little girl!

If you could design a giant structure, what would you build?

Frederick William Stevens began designing the terminus in 1878, and today, 140 years later, we are still using and admiring this beautiful building. If you could design a building which will last for hundreds of years, what would you build?

Plan a long train journey through India, seeing as many places as possible!

India has one of the most extensive railway networks in the world. From north to south and east to west, over rivers and under mountains, many parts of the country are connected by long, winding railways. What are the places you would like to see during this journey?

If you could work on something for 38 years, what would it be?

Bandu, the time-keeper in our story, is based on BK Jadhav, who was the real time-keeper at CST for thirty-eight years! He took care of nearly 900 clocks for many years because he loved his job so much. If you could have a job which you had to do for 38 years, what would you choose to do?

First published in India in 2018 by

Mapin Publishing Pvt. Ltd
706 Kaivanna, Panchvati, Ellisbridge
Ahmedabad 380006 INDIA
T: +91 79 40 228 228
F: +91 79 40 228 201
E: mapin@mapinpub.com
www.mapinpub.com

International Distribution

Worldwide (except North America and South Asia)
Prestel Publishing Ltd.
14-17 Wells Street
London W1T 3PD
T: +44 (0)20 7323 5004
F: +44 (0)20 7323 0271
E: sales@prestel-uk.co.uk

North America
Antique Collectors' Club
T: +1 800 252 5231
F: +1 413 529 0862
E: sales@accpublishinggroup.com
www.accpublishinggroup.com/us

South Asia
Mapin Publishing Pvt. Ltd

ISBN: 978-93-85360-51-0
Series ISBN: 978-93-85360-47-3

Series Editor: Narayani Gupta
Copyediting: Mithila Rangarajan / Mapin Editorial
Design and Production:
Gopal Limbad, Darshit Mori /
Mapin Design Studio

Printed in India

The creation of this book was supported by Parag, an initiative of TATA Trusts.

parag
AN INITIATIVE OF TATA TRUSTS

Author: **Subuhi Jiwani** walked into Bombay's historic buildings by chance and fell in love with them. Recently, she narrated the story of one such building—and its people—on video. She has found that the stories of these buildings are endless. She returns to them again and again to learn more about her city's history and her own childlike awe.

Artist: **Kishan Dev** has worked for a lot of blockbuster Bollywood movies and TV series but his real love is drawing and storytelling. He once went to Florence, Italy to study oil painting, and is now exploring the French techniques of plein-air painting with his friends. He loves to paint outdoors and also to encourage others to sketch!

Artist: **Gopal Limbad** heads the design team at Mapin and he has helped make the Roshni books look beautiful. He loves art and has a degree in Fine Art from M.S. University in Vadodara. Gopal collaborated with Kishan to create the illustrations on the cover and inside cover page, as well as on pages 9, 13, 14–15, 19 (left), 22–23, 27 and 28.